To David and to Lucy
with love

The correspondence in this book is a work of fiction.
The name Greenpeace is used by kind permission of
Greenpeace UK, Canonbury Villas,
London N1 2PN

First published 1991 by
Walker Books Ltd, 87 Vauxhall Walk
London SE11 5HJ

6 8 10 9 7 5

Printed in Hong Kong

British Library Cataloguing in Publication Data
A catalogue record for this book is
available from the British Library.

ISBN 0-7445-1536-X

Dear Greenpeace

SIMON JAMES

WALKER BOOKS
AND SUBSIDIARIES
LONDON • BOSTON • SYDNEY

Dear Greenpeace,

   I love whales very much and
I think I saw one in my pond
today. Please send me some
information on whales, as
I think he might be hurt.

       Love
       Emily

Dear Emily,

  Here are some details about whales. I don't think you'll find it was a whale you saw, because whales don't live in ponds, but in salt water.

     Yours sincerely,
     Greenpeace

Dear Greenpeace,

I am now putting salt into the pond every day before school and last night I saw my whale smile. I think he is feeling better. Do you think he might be lost?

Love
Emily

Dear Emily,

   Please don't put any more salt in the pond, I'm sure your parents won't be pleased.

   I'm afraid there can't be a whale in your pond, because whales don't get lost, they always know where they are in the oceans.

Yours sincerely,
Greenpeace

Dear Greenpeace,

Tonight I am very happy because I saw my whale jump up and spurt lots of water. He looked blue.

Does this mean he might be a blue whale?

Love
Emily

P. S. What can I feed him with?

Dear Emily,

Blue whales are blue and they eat tiny shrimp-like creatures that live in the sea. However I must tell you that a blue whale is much too big to live in your pond.

Yours sincerely,

Greenpeace

P.S. Perhaps it is a blue goldfish?

Dear Greenpeace,

Last night I read your letter to my whale. Afterwards he let me stroke his head. It was very exciting.

I secretly took him some crunched-up cornflakes and bread-crumbs. This morning I looked in the pond and they were all gone!

I think I shall call him Arthur, what do you think?

Love
Emily

Dear Emily,

I must point out to you quite forcefully now that in no way could a whale live in your pond. You may not know that whales are migratory, which means they travel great distances each day.

I am sorry to disappoint you.

Yours sincerely,
Greenpeace

Dear Greenpeace,
   Tonight I'm a little sad. Arthur has gone. I think your letter made sense to him and he has decided to be migratory again.

Love
Emily

Dear Emily,

   Please don't be too sad, it really was impossible for a whale to live in your pond. Perhaps when you are older you would like to sail the oceans studying and protecting whales with us.

   Yours sincerely,
   Greenpeace

Dear Greenpeace,

It's been the happiest day!
I went to the seaside and you'll
never guess, but I saw Arthur!
I called to him and he smiled.
I knew it was Arthur because
he let me stroke his head.

I gave him some of my
sandwich...

and then we said goodbye.
  I shouted that I loved him very
much and, I hope you don't mind,
I said you loved him too.

      love
        Emily (and Arthur)

The End